A Planet Called Home

Eco-Pig's Animal Protection

By Lisa S. French

Illustrations by Barry Gott

visit us at www.abdopublishing.com

Charalambos and Thalia—LSF

Published by Magic Wagon, a division of the ABDO Group, 8000 West 78th Street, Edina, Minnesota 55439.

Looking Glass Library™ is a trademark and logo of Magic Wagon.

Printed in the United States.

 Manufactured with paper containing at least 10% post-consumer waste

Text by Lisa S. French
Illustrations by Barry Gott
Edited by Stephanie Hedlund and Rochelle Baltzer
Interior layout and design by Nicole Brecke
Cover design by Nicole Brecke

Library of Congress Cataloging-in-Publication Data
French, Lisa S.
  A planet called home : Eco-Pig's animal protection / by Lisa S. French ; illustrated by Barry Gott.
    p. cm. — (Eco-Pig)
  Summary: In rhyming text, Eco-Pig and his friends discover visitors in their town of To-Be whose homes had been demolished by mankind.
  ISBN 978-1-60270-662-0
  [1. Stories in rhyme. 2. Pigs—Fiction. 3. Animals—Fiction. 4. Wildlife conservation—Fiction. 5. Environmental protection—Fiction. 6. Green movement—Fiction.] I. Gott, Barry, ill. II. Title.
  PZ8.3.F9085Pl 2009
  [E]—dc22
                          2008055339

Eco-Pig pedaled
through the town of To-Be.
His two very best friends joined him
on a bicycle for three.

They rolled past the wind farm
and the Green Goodies Shop.
But they stepped on the brakes
at the electric bus stop.

E.P. stood and he stared.

So did Lou and McGee.

E.P. asked his two friends,

"Do you see what I see?"

There was a family of polar bears,
a black-footed ferret or two,
a sea otter, and a gray wolf.
"Where did you come from?" cried Lou.

"We came on the bus," said Pat Polar.

"We've been riding all day.

We've all lost our homes.

We need someplace to stay!"

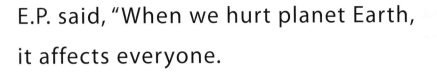

E.P. said, "When we hurt planet Earth,
it affects everyone.
All people, pigs, and polar bears,
every creature under the sun."

"We lived on a prairie," sighed Fred Ferret.

"What a great place to roam!

Since it's turned into farmland,

we have no place to call home!"

9

"And the sea ice is melting," said Pat,
"out from under our feet.
That makes fishing too hard!
Now we have nothing to eat!"

Olive Otter added, "I floated
right into a big oil spill.
I tell you that water pollution
makes this poor otter ill!"

"I'm George," said the gray wolf.
"I need a place to run free.
Without a wide-open space,
it's so hard to be me!"

"With no place to live," said E.P.,
"wolves could be gone forever!
We can't let that happen,
we all have to say never!

13

"If I came back from recycling,
and my tree was not there,
and my apples were gone,
that sure wouldn't be fair.

"Every creature on Earth
should have a good life.
That includes Fred Ferret
and Betty, his wife.

"Every sea otter,
every great polar bear,
and George the gray wolf
all need us to care!

"We all can have homes
and enough food to eat,
if we look out for each other.
Wouldn't that be neat!?"

17

"Let's turn down the heat," said Pat.
"What a great way to start!
If you help stop global warming,
it shows you have heart!"

Cooler

Warmer

You can walk, ride a bike,
or take a bus to your school.
The fewer cars on the road,
the more Earth stays cool!

"I have a favor to ask," Olive said.
"Please don't pollute water!
Remember somebody lives there,
and it just might be an otter!

"When you go for a swim,
don't leave trash on the beach.
Keep soda cans, plastic bottles,
and plastic bags out of reach."

"And if you obey special laws
that make our homes a safe place,"
said George, "I'll howl at the moon
with a grin on my face!"

ANIMAL 🐾
SANCTUARY

"Wherever we are," E.P. said,
"there are creatures nearby.
We have friends on the land,
in the sea, and in the sky!

"Let's try to remember
that each thing we do
could save a friend's life.
Believe me, it's true!

"Learn as much as you can
about each habitat.
Help guard them from danger.
I'd really like that!"

25

"Excuse me, kind sir,"
Fred Ferret said to E.P.
"If we're quiet and neat,
may we live in To-Be?"

"Of course you can live here,
but first you should eat!
Let's all go to the diner!
I'm buying, my treat."

27

Everyone got fresh fish.

They shared green peppers and peas.

When offered green apple pie,

they all nodded and said, "Please!"

Olive smiled and said, "Thank you, E.P.
What a great day!
Now To-Be is our home,
a friendly, safe place to stay!"

Words to Know

ecology—relations between organisms and their environment.

electric bus—a bus powered by clean electric energy that does not pollute the air.

global warming—an average increase in Earth's temperature, which in turn causes changes in climate.

habitat—the place where an animal normally lives and grows.

oil spill—when oil has leaked into the ocean from an oil tanker.

pollute—to contaminate the environment with man-made waste.

recycle—to break down waste, glass, or cans so they can be used again.

wind farm—a group of machines that convert wind into electrical energy.

Did You Know?

- Every year, 27,000 animal species become extinct.

- One in four animals is in danger of becoming extinct.

- Many species disappear because their homes disappear and they are not able to move to a new environment.

- The leading causes of habitat destruction are:
    a. Clearing wilderness to create farmland.
    b. Pollution, which destroys ecosystems and habitats.
    c. Burning fossil fuels, which contributes to global warming, causing ice to melt and sea levels to rise.
    d. Clearing forests for lumber and firewood.

- All living things are a part of the chain of nature.

- If one animal disappears, we may not notice, but it can change Earth's ecosystem.

More Ways to Make Our Planet Animal Friendly!

Talk to your mom and dad about what you can try at home:

1. Learn as much as you can about endangered animals.
2. Treat wildlife with respect. Don't disturb nests or natural habitats near your home.
3. Set up birdbaths and bird feeders.
4. Plant flowers, trees, and shrubs to attract birds, bees, and butterflies.
5. Don't dump trash into the gutter or the streets. It will end up in rivers, lakes, and streams.
6. Pick up plastic bags at the beach. If swallowed they can kill turtles, dolphins, otters, and other marine life.
7. Cut up six-pack rings from soda and juice cans. Animals can swallow or become trapped in them.